CHAPTER ONE
Oliver's Collection

It all started with a tooth – a very large tooth. Oliver spotted it while he was busy searching for fossils on the beach with Tilly.

"What's this?" he asked, holding the strange thing in the air.

"It looks like a tooth!" said his sister.

"It's a dinosaur's tooth," explained Mum.

"Wow!" cried Oliver.

"That's cool."

W
FRANKLIN WATTS
LONDON•SYDNEY

The tooth was smooth and bigger than Oliver's finger. One end was pointed and the other was jagged and looked like it had been broken.

"It's huge!" said Tilly.

"Some dinosaurs' teeth were even bigger than that," said Mum.

Oliver couldn't wait to get home. As soon as they got there he raced up to his room, took his old fossil box out from under his bed and emptied the fossils onto the floor. Then he carefully placed the dinosaur tooth inside the box.

OLIVER'S FOSSILS

KEEP OUT

6

"I'm not collecting fossils anymore," Oliver announced. "I'm collecting teeth." Dad laughed. "You'll have a long time to wait," he said. "It's not every day that you find a tooth."

But Dad had been wrong. Oliver found another one the very next day, lying on the kitchen floor next to Biscuit's food bowl.

"But Biscuit's only a kitten," said Oliver. "He shouldn't be losing his teeth."

"Don't worry," Mum reassured him. "It's only a milk tooth."

"Biscuit won't end up like Grandma, will he?" asked Tilly, looking worried. Grandma had false teeth that she took out at night. Sometimes she took them out during the day too and forgot where she had left them. "Kittens lose their milk teeth the same way we do," said Mum. "Then they are replaced by their adult teeth."

After that, Oliver became very interested in teeth. If he wasn't reading about them in a book he was examining his own teeth in the bathroom mirror.

He was eager to learn how teeth grew and why they fell out. Before, Mum had always had to nag Oliver to brush his teeth. Now he brushed them first thing in the morning and last thing at night. He even took his toothbrush to school so he could brush them at lunchtime.

CHAPTER TWO
Mr Scrape

As time went by, Oliver's collection of teeth grew and grew. Teeth of all shapes and sizes filled the shelves in his bedroom. Uncle Bryn even brought him a set of shark's teeth back from Australia. Oliver thought they were awesome.

Spike didn't think the teeth were awesome.

He growled at them, then hid behind the

sofa and refused to come out.

Oliver showed the teeth to Tilly but she

didn't think they were awesome either.

"Stop teasing your sister," said Mum.

Even though not everyone liked Oliver's collection, Mr and Mrs Payne were delighted their son had a new interest. It was the first time he had shown interest in anything apart from playing games and watching cartoons.

"I think he'll grow up to be a doctor," said Mr Payne proudly. "Just like me."

But after watching Dad at work, Oliver knew that being a doctor was not for him. He liked the idea of making people better but there were lots of things that he didn't like. Doctors had to deal with lots of squishy things and Oliver didn't like that at all.

"No!" said Mrs Payne. "I think he will grow up to be a vet like me." This sounded much better. Oliver loved animals and the thought of being able to help sick and injured animals seemed perfect. But after following Mum around he soon changed his mind. There were some things about being a vet that were definitely not for him.

It wasn't until they visited Mr Scrape that Oliver realised something. Mr Scrape's room was sparkling and clean. Oliver gazed at the row of shiny dentist tools neatly laid out on Mr Scrape's table. He relaxed in Mr Scrape's comfortable chair as the dentist peered into his mouth.

DRILL-O-MATIC

Oliver could hardly wait for it to be Dad's turn in the chair.

"Are you going to use the drill?" he asked excitedly.

Dad pulled a funny face and nearly fell off the chair but Mr Scrape shook his head.

"No," he reassured him. "Just a check-up."

As Dad sighed with relief, Oliver couldn't help feeling disappointed. He loved the sound of Mr Scrape's drill. Oliver didn't stay disappointed for long and when they got home he had something to say.

"I'm going to be a dentist!" announced Oliver Payne.

CHAPTER THREE
Open Wide

Mr and Mrs Payne could hardly believe their ears.

"But I thought you wanted to help people," said Dad.

"And I thought you wanted to help animals," said Mum.

"I do!" insisted Oliver.

"So why on Earth do you want to be a DENTIST?" they cried.

"Not a normal dentist," explained Oliver. "I want to be a dentist for humans AND animals." Oliver found out that learning to be a dentist would take years, so there was no time to waste.

For his birthday, Oliver got a brand new

dentist chair.

"Are you sure this is what you want?"

asked Dad.

"Definitely!" said Oliver. "Do you want

a go?"

"No thanks!" cried Dad, disappearing

back down the stairs.

When Oliver got home from school the

next day, Spike was sitting in his new chair.

"Get down from there," said Oliver.

Spike ignored him and licked his face.

"Yuk!" cried Oliver. "Your breath stinks."

Suddenly, Oliver's eyes lit up.

"My first patient!" he cried excitedly.

"Wait right there."

Oliver rushed into the bathroom and grabbed Dad's toothbrush. He gave it a squirt of 'Gleam-O-Jell' toothpaste. Then he stuck the toothbrush into Spike's mouth. "Open wide!" said Oliver. Spike didn't seem to like having his teeth brushed. As soon as Oliver had finished, he leapt out of the dentist chair spraying toothpaste everywhere.

While Spike raced off to find a drink of water, Oliver put Dad's toothbrush back and went in search of his next patient. He didn't have far to look. Mum had found Grandma's false teeth in the garden. They're filthy," said Mum.

"Don't worry," said Oliver. "I can fix that for you. Sparkle and Shine washing-up liquid should do the trick."

In no time at all, Grandma's teeth were sparkling and shining like new. Grandma wasn't so sure though.

"I think I've mastered the cleaning part of the job," he said. "I'm ready for some real dentist work now."

Oliver found Tilly sitting on her bed with Mr Wibbles and a big frown.

"What's up?" he asked.

"I've got a wobbly tooth," moaned his sister.

Oliver grinned. Today was turning out to be the best day of his life. At this rate he would be a proper dentist in no time.

"Don't worry!" said Oliver. "I can fix that
for you."

As Oliver's bedroom door slammed,
Tilly screamed.

"That was the wrong tooth!" she howled.

"Oops!" said Oliver.

CHAPTER FOUR
Celebrity Smiles

Mum and Dad thought Oliver's dream of being a dentist for humans and animals was silly. But they were wrong. People loved having their teeth polished at the same time as their pampered pets.

It wasn't long before everyone knew about Oliver Payne, and celebrities from around the world came to him night and day.

The princess of pop, Kelly Minnow, brought her dogs for a polish and shine.

"Pippy and Poppy look positively perfect now," she smiled.

Hollywood hunk, Dack Timber, brought his pet python.

"Poor little Monty has something stuck between his teeth," moaned Dack.

"Don't worry!" said Oliver. "I can fix that for you." Not an hour passed by without someone knocking on his door.

One of the things that made Oliver so popular was his great invention – 'Dazzle' – a toothpaste that not only polished and whitened, but made your teeth really dazzle. Every tube of the amazing stuff came with three things:

1. A warning – 'May blind people when you smile.'
2. A pair of dark sunglasses.
3. A guarantee to 'DAZZLE' or your money back.

Oliver loved his job and worked so hard that he hardly had time to sleep. One day, he nodded off whilst filling a hole in the Lord Mayor's molars.

Another time, Oliver started snoring whilst straightening the Prime Minister's canines.

There were pictures of Oliver in the papers every day and it wasn't long before he was the busiest dentist in the world. Patients had to wait months just to get an appointment. Tilly tried helping out but it wasn't easy. The telephone never stopped ringing and there wasn't a moment's peace.

One evening, Tilly unplugged the phone and hung a closed sign on the door.

"You can't do that!" cried Oliver. "What about my patients?"

"Never mind them," said Tilly. "You need some sleep."

"No I don't" said Oliver. "I'm perfectly ..." But Oliver didn't finish his words. He was already snoring soundly.

While he slept, a man walked in carrying a silver tray.

"Sorry!" whispered Tilly, "but we're closed." The man raised one eyebrow and lifted the lid off the tray. Beneath it lay a golden mobile phone. Before Tilly could speak it began to ring. She recognised the ringtone right away. It was the British National Anthem, *God Save the Queen*.

"I believe it's for you Miss," said the man.

CHAPTER FIVE
A Royal Calling

Tilly held the phone to her ear.

Suddenly her eyes sprang wide open.

"Yes, Your Majesty. Of course Your Highness.

Right away Your Royal Majesty Highness."

said Tilly, sounding very flustered.

"There's no need to curtsey," said the man.

"Her Majesty can't see you."

"Sorry!" said Tilly.

"No time for apologies," said the man. "Her Majesty doesn't like to be kept waiting."

Oliver was half asleep when they pushed him into the back of the royal car.

"This is the Queen's butler," Tilly explained. "Her Royal Highness needs us."

Oliver was suddenly wide awake.

"The Q-Q-Queen!" he stuttered.

"It's a matter of urgency," said the butler.

"You mean Her Majesty wants me to fix her teeth?" said Oliver.

"Certainly not," said the butler. "Her Majesty's teeth are perfect."

"It's Princess Gertrude's teeth,"
explained Tilly.

"And her pony's teeth," added the butler.

As they drove to the palace, Tilly and the
royal butler explained everything.

"The princess wanted to practise for a showjumping competition but they had a little accident. They were so excited that they galloped out of the stables," said the royal butler.

"But someone forgot to open the stable doors properly," added Tilly.

"Crunch!" said the royal butler, holding up a plastic bag.

"Ouch!" groaned Oliver. The bag was full of teeth. "Don't worry," he said "I can fix that."

"You have until tomorrow morning," said the royal butler, "before the competition starts."

"But that's impossible!" cried Oliver.

The butler just smiled. "Bramble and Princess Gertrude are waiting in the royal surgery," he said.

41

Oliver worked all night drilling and filling, capping and fixing, polishing and shining.

Tilly's job was to keep Oliver awake.

She prodded him when he started snoring with the drill.

She poked him when he fell asleep staring into the pony's mouth.

43

As the night went on, Oliver got the feeling something wasn't quite right, but he was too tired to think what. As soon as he had finished, Oliver fell fast asleep and didn't wake up again until the following morning.

"Look at this!" demanded the royal butler.

"Her Royal Majesty is not amused"

Oliver looked at the newspaper and gasped.

"They won everything," said Tilly.

"But look at their teeth," cried the butler.

Oliver realised what he had done wrong.
He had put the wrong teeth into the wrong
mouths. Now, Princess Gertrude had huge
pony teeth and Bramble had the princess's
teeth.

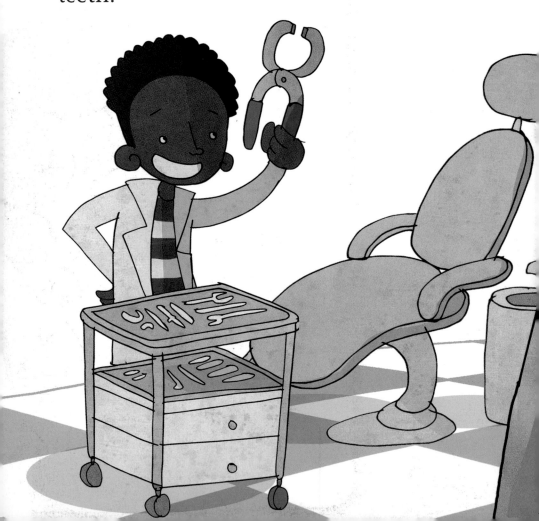

"It's a disaster!" cried the royal butler.

"Don't worry," smiled Oliver. "I can fix that for you."

Franklin Watts
First published in Great Britain in 2016 by
The Watts Publishing Group

Text © Damian Harvey 2016
Illustrations © Ben Scruton 2016

Series Editor: Melanie Palmer
Series Advisor: Catherine Glavina
Cover Designer: Cathryn Gilbert
Design Manager: Peter Scoulding

ISBN 978 1 4451 5000 0 (hbk)
ISBN 978 1 4451 5002 4 (pbk)
ISBN 978 1 4451 5001 7 (library ebook)

Printed in China

Franklin Watts
An imprint of
Hachette Children's Group
Part of The Watts Publishing Group
Carmelite House
50 Victoria Embankment
London EC4Y 0DZ

An Hachette UK Company
www.hachette.co.uk

www.franklinwatts.co.uk

FSC
www.fsc.org

MIX
Paper from
responsible sources
FSC® C104740